Zizi and Tish

Dewdney Elementary School
Books for Breakfast
April 2006

ORCA BOOK PUBLISHERS

National Library of Canada Cataloguing in Publication Data

Moore, Liz, 1959—

Zizi and Tish / Liz Moore ; [illustrations by] Liz Milkau.

ISBN 1-55143-254-4

1. Sisters—Juvenile fiction. I. Milkau, Liz. II. Title.

PS8576.061445Z29 2003   jC813'.6   C2002-911188-9

PZ7.M7866Zi 2003

First published in the United States, 2003

Library of Congress Control Number: 2002113293

Summary: Zizi thinks her summer at the cottage with her sister is perfect until a girl from across the lake lures Tish away, leaving Zizi to entertain herself.

Teacher's guide available from Orca Book Publishers.

Orca Book Publishers gratefully acknowledges the support of its publishing programs provided by the following agencies: the Department of Canadian Heritage, the Canada Council for the Arts, and the British Columbia Arts Council.

Design by Christine Toller
Printed and bound in Hong Kong

IN CANADA:
Orca Book Publishers
1030 North Park Street
Victoria, BC Canada
V8T 1C6

IN THE UNITED STATES:
Orca Book Publishers
PO Box 468
Custer, WA USA
98240-0468

05 04 03 • 5 4 3 2 1

Zizi and Tish

written by **Liz Moore**

illustrated by **Liz Milkau**

For Tish and Marn — with thanks — for continuing to see me through the thunder.

LIZ MOORE

For Mom, Dad, G&G and Steve.

LIZ MILKAU

Zizi and Tish were sisters. They had long, chocolate-colored ponytails and cinnamon freckles across their noses.

Zizi was the small one. She liked holding hands and hiding in tiny, just-her-size places.

Tish was the tall one. She knew how to buy things in stores and ride a two-wheeler.

At the cottage, Zizi and Tish picked blueberries for pie. They swung high on the tire swing that hung from the pine tree that stood like a tower in the woods. They pretended they were lost in the jungle and made houses from branches off the forest floor. The tree stumps were their thrones.

Zizi dabbled her toes in the lake.

"Come on in!" Tish called. "I bet you could make it all the way to the raft!"

"Too deep," Zizi said.

Instead, the girls made villages of sand huts and waded up to their knees, searching for keeper stones, jewels, in the sand under the water.

"Hi!" said a voice.

A girl with short, spiky hair the color of rust stood on the dock. She was as tall as Tish. Fluorescent wristbands twisted around her arms like Slinkies.

"I'm Kimber," said the girl. "I'm visiting my aunt across the bay. She thought you might be twelve like me."

Zizi thought that the girl's name sounded like hammers.

Tish dropped her pebbles and stepped past Zizi, stirring up sand and water and jewels.

Zizi gathered berries alone, bending and picking.

"That's not enough for a pie," her mom said. "We'll have them on ice cream instead."

On her tree-stump throne, Zizi worked with her paper and markers. *Water skeeing is laym*, she wrote in bright red letters and put the note under a rock on the path.

Kimber and Tish climbed trees in the forest and sat high up on branches, singing songs from the radio and looking down on the cottages and the lake and Zizi. They put barrettes in each other's hair and tried on each other's clothes. They made peanut-butter-and-potato-chip sandwiches to take on long hikes in the woods.

Zizi hung on tight to the tire swing and imagined living upside down at the top of a forest, walking on the underside of branches to get around.

"C'mon, Zeez!" Tish called from out on the lake where the water was bottomless and dark.

Zizi peered out at the jostling waves.

"She's even afraid of the top bunk," Tish told Kimber.

"Is she afraid of everything?" asked Kimber, laughing and disappearing under the water.

Tish cant evn flot on a ayr mattress, Zizi wrote on another piece of paper and put it in Tish's shoe.

In the evening, they toasted marshmallows over the fire. The bigger girls held their sticks far from the coals. Zizi pushed her stick into the yellow flames. She watched, fascinated, as the marshmallows blazed and turned crusty black, then knocked them off into the fire.

"Eewwww," squealed the older girls. "Don't do that!"

Kimber's earrings swung as the two of them snickered like witches.

Who wears earrings at a cottage? Zizi thought.

When the sun dropped behind the trees, the lapping lake whispered, "Goodnight . . . goodnight."

And Zizi's mom whispered, "Time for bed, little one."

Zizi snuggled into her cozy bunk and reached for her markers. *Tish is sucky and a chiken bayby*, she wrote and let the bit of paper flutter under her curtain, out into the big room, where Tish and Kimber sprawled in their sleeping bags like seals.

Flick, flick went the pages of their magazines. Zizi made the worst face she could think of, worse than liver. *Kimber and Tish are stoopidstar lip-sick dorks. Thay are so NOT kool*, she wrote and folded the corners so that the paper could fly.

Flick, giggle, flick.

Zizi crawled back into bed and floated to sleep to the grownups' murmuring voices.

Zizi woke up.

Far away, she heard rumbling. It started low, but soon it rolled across the sky and growled right over their cottage. All at once, the world lit up, white and haunted.

A furious slap smacked the air around her and shook her bed.

Zizi wanted to call her mother, but her voice was too scared to come out. This was worse than the top bunk. Or the deep water.

Thunder boomed, stinging her ears. Lightning flashed. Zizi shrank into her blankets, but the trampling of rain on the roof pushed right into her bunk.

Zizi was as alone as the raft on the black lake.

"Zizi, are you okay?"

It was Tish!

"I'm scared," said Zizi.

"Me too. Come on."

"Where's Kimber?"

"Still asleep. Come on."

Tish's hand was cool and dry. Zizi squeezed her fingers, climbed out of bed on quivery legs and padded along behind her brave, grown-up sister.

Blasts bashed at the walls as they made their way out to the screened porch. The air smelled like leaves and wet dirt. They climbed onto the high wooden spare bed. Tish pulled a heavy blanket over the two of them and they shivered, watching the lake and sky.

Spiders of lightning crisscrossed the sky like fireworks and glittered on the restless water. Sturdy trees bowed in the wind. Wild thunder-cracks made the girls jump and squeal and laugh until they were limp.

The rain poured on. They pretended they were in the woods, dry in their home of branches and moss.

Then, it passed. The thunder tired itself out and became faraway drumbeats. The rain-rush slowed to a trickle, a dribble, drips, a sniff.

The breeze sighed and whisked the girls' hair across their faces.

Tish and Zizi fell asleep in the spare bed on the screened porch, while the lapping lake whispered, "Goodnight . . . goodnight."

The next day Zizi did up her life jacket, closed her eyes . . . counted to seven and a half . . . and . . . plunged in!

"Go, Zeez-girl!"

Zizi felt nothingness beneath her feet. It was cushiony and slippery. It swirled around her wriggling arms and legs like Jell-O and held her, lifted her up when she kicked. It moved when she pushed it and splashed around her. It got up her nose.

Zizi and Tish and Kimber floated on their backs and pretended they were walking on the underside of clouds.

Then, while her mom and dad watched from the dock and Tish and Kimber swam on either side, Zizi dog-paddled away from the dock, out into the lake. She pushed and pulled her hands and feet and swam all the way to the raft.

Zizi pulled herself up onto the wet wood and stood on the raft like a star on a stage.

At bedtime, a tiny knob of paper sat on Zizi's pillow. Inside the rolled-up letter, the pink words said — *Sleep tight, superstar.*